DARPA
SPACE

MANUEL PELAEZ

Darpa Space by Manuel Pelaez

ISBN 978-1-952027-30-7 (Paperback)
ISBN 978-1-952027-31-4 (Hardback)

This book is written to provide information and motivation to readers. Its purpose is not to render any type of psychological, legal, or professional advice of any kind. The content is the sole opinion and expression of the author, and not necessarily that of the publisher.

Printed in the United States of America.

New Leaf Media, LLC
175 S. 3rd Street, Suite 200
Columbus, OH 43215
www.thenewleafmedia.com

DARPA

SPACE

INTRODUCTION

It is my pleasure to introduce my written masterpiece. In this project (DARPA space) volume 4, I managed to harvest the energy of the trilogy DARPA genesis, DARPA mesial, DARPA cataclysm, and create this magnificent book. All questions are answered, all doubts are vanished, it is a wild ride that doesn't let go. The birth of future projects emerges for futures to come, enjoy everyone.

CHAPTER 1

After several months gone by and every federal agencies (Nuclear Emergency Support Team) NEST, (The Centers for Disease Control) CDC, (Department of Homeland Security) DHA, (Federal Emergency Management Agency) FEMA, and other top secret agencies all in hazmat suits, joined by scientists and other experts in their respected fields. Not to mention a global investigation at unprecedented levels to find answers to what caused the single lost of life ever on United States soil. This overwhelming sorrow is felt throughout our world, hundreds of thousands of civilians, military personals, government officials, this day marks the single most devastating incident ever caused by a blast of immense destructive energy. Never since World War 2, such sorrow has been felt throughout our world, absolutely everyone on Earth is in complete shock and in tears. Almost all areas of Virginia are being evacuated, countless of dead bodies and the world is working 24/7 to find the living in all this chaos. Entire regions were put into quarantine, massive tent cities were created to somehow salvage them from what awakes them radiation poisoning. So many bodies death is displayed everywhere and sadly almost all the victims exposed to the high levels of radiation will not survive. To work in this environment worker's most definitely need strong stomachs, as the months followed a endless list of victims was carefully composed. Month after month on several large screens posted outside in safe zones away from the toxic radiation zones and quarantine tent cities, displaying all the victims that perished in the blast. The victims are predicted in the hundreds of thousands, every month the suffering is to much to bear for the survivors, families, friends, basically the entire world. Many countries have posted several large screens displaying the victims also and to serve as a reminder to all humanity on how horrific this tragedy event truly was. People all over the world are constantly in tears and the sorrow is reflected everywhere. The list of victims is getting bigger as the months pass by, because many victims inside the quarantine tent cities die from radiation poisoning.

CHAPTER 2

While, all these events were occurring between the investigation of what exactly happened and televising all the victims of this horrific accident, something was happening back in Africa inside the forbidden underground cities. When the horrific accident occurred Marcus (Izem) heart was shattered, he continuously was mourning with his family, but can participate in the discussions whenever he feels up to it. Director Jones, knows what is ahead will be extremely challenging, he gathers with the special ones the two kids (Whit and Shu) from the late Zon, and the team of robotic engineer scientists. Director Jones begins saying, we need to put together a future plan for DARPA, First, I need to get in contact with my trusted colleagues if any are still alive. Second, we need to built a plague memorial of the heroes that gave their lives for DARPA's future. Third, we need to set up some kind of memorial service for all the victims that past away from this horrific accident, and honor them in some way. Fourth, Whit and Shu shall gather all the special ones that are spread throughout our world to create a better DARPA and salvage our precious creatures coming up with creative solutions. Fifth, we will use DARPA's advance technologies and scientific breakthroughs to achieve the goal of stopping the slaughter of our innocent creatures both land and sea. Sixth, we will make an accurate account of what members are still alive like cadets and other personal from our previous DARPA. Seventh, we need to make this effort worldwide getting everyone on board by many countries joining together to protect our Earth's creatures and stop further deterioration of our world. Everyone is in agreement with the discussions hoping for a better DARPA to be formed. After waiting for the right time to reappear back to civilization, the day finally came where the dark lord's (donkere here), inside the forbidden underground cities covered up each member of the group to escort them outside in a designated area. Once, the group were outside the dark lord's (donkere here), took off the head covers and disappeared like ghost. Now, Whit uses his telepathic abilities to summon a herd of African elephants, as they are waiting they make a plan to get to nearest phone where Director Jones can reach out to his colleagues.

Chapter 3

At a distance, the group can see the herd of elephants as they are all following a massive bull elephant. Whit, can't believe it is (TOTO), ever since the animals and sea creatures were freed from (UNÍ-WORLD), the reunions will be formed once again. Whit, hugs (TOTO) standing at 13 feet in height, weighing in at several tons, with tusks of 7 feet long. (TOTO) lowers himself and the rest of the herd do the same to allow each group member to sit on their backs. The journey begins now to find a village or town with a phone that has an outside line for Director Jones to make contact and make arrangements for the group to get picked up. Since, the Massive Space Energy Sphere left our galaxy they restored the Earth's energy grinds, but disabling the nuclear weapon capabilities because of the dangers humanity poses on itself. After traveling many miles they find a small town that seems to have a working phone. It's a small hotel that seemed abandoned but there were some people inside and by the look in their faces it reflects the changes that went on to a more darker side. The stories are endless everywhere you go about how everything was taken over and the population was placed into re-evaluation zones, then everything went dark, no electricity, nothing worked, it was like living in the stone ages. The group hears their individual stories while Director Jones continuously reached out to his colleagues to see if anyone is still alive. Finally, Director Jones gets through to one of his colleagues when he gives him the bad news of Congressman Whitman being executed along with others that he knew so well. Director Jones, drops to the ground in tears, with the phone still in his hand. The group goes to his aid and they themselves are heart-broken also. Director Jones, knows he must be strong, and tells everyone he's alright to continue. Director Jones, tells the group that we need to get to the airfield closes to us because a cargo plane will come for us and after we land we will figure out everything including their love ones. The group gets back on track to the nearest airfield which they determined where exactly that is and plans are made before their decent. The group quickly wastes no time and begin their travel on the backs of the African elephants towards the airfield.

CHAPTER 4

Director Jones, is only living highest member of the previous administration top secret program called DARPA, others survived like the cadets, and other members that didn't pose any threats, but from the top brass only he was able to survive by fleeing and going into hiding. After many days traveling towards the airfield, when the group arrives the military cargo plane is already there waiting for them. Whit, hugs (TOTO) once again to say there goodbyes (he tells the massive bull elephant I'll see you again my friend). The entire group one by one board the plane, Director Jones, Whit, Shu, Marcus, Julie, their twin daughters, and the four robotic engineering scientists team. A strict gag order is in place for all military personal to talk about previous events, or any other sensitive materials. Once, airborne the military personnel tell the group they will be landing in Texas (a unknown destination), where accommodations are waiting for them to relax, shower, food, clean clothes. Afterwards, Director Jones will brief everyone on how to move forward with the future of DARPA. Further accommodations will also be done for the entire group because their previous homes were destroyed by the vicious administration of a darker DARPA.

CHAPTER 5

Upon landing, the group were set up in their living quarters were they can get much needed rest, shower, food, clean clothes. Once, a couple of days went by the group has so many questions about their love ones, colleagues, and exactly the extent of the horrific accident. A representative of the military told the entire group that all their questions were going to be answered the next morning in a meeting. The next morning, everyone took a seat in the conference room, with a large monitor on the wall, charts, data, and classified information. The group were accompanied by military personnel including psychologist, and healthcare staff, the talks begin, the entire rural areas of Virginia were completely wiped out. The radiation spread into some urban areas, the death toll was approximately in the hundreds of thousands of lives. We have many quarantine tent cities trying to give comfort to those victims exposed, but many are dying. The entire previous administration of DARPA were executed, including Congressman Whitman and all other top military officials. Most of the other staff that weren't seen as any threat were spared like the cadets, and the biologists, some scientists, mechanical engineers, etc. Some of the re-relocation zones survived the blast because they were at safe distances, especially the children. Many did not survive the blast Including the entire group called the (inner circle) and their military personnel loyalists. Let's make everything crystal clear, the reason why the entire (inner circle) and military loyalists which were the high command of everyone in the military in many countries not just the United States, were all gathered together was for the big event about to take place, where the (zero point energy manual cannons) were about to open fire on the Massive Space Energy Sphere, but the horrific accident occurred when the massive cannons were being calibrated to fire on a target in space.

CHAPTER 6

At this time we regret to inform you that one of your robotic scientist family was killed by the blast. The minute this was mentioned by the military personnel, the military psychologist told scientist Ron Ben Ruckman to please come with them. The scientist drops to the floor crying (NO, NO, NO), the rest of the group try to help him up, he kept saying out loud (my wife was pregnant), it was difficult to watch. He was safely removed from the conference room and placed with the military psychologist and healthcare personnel to ease his pain. Director Jones, was also in pain losing all his colleagues and friends, the entire group is mourning. Director Jones, knows that the entire world is counting on him and he must show restraint and courage moving forward. The military personnel and the group agree that DARPA's future is at stake and they need to rebuild a new DARPA. Marcus and his family shall have another home for them wherever they agree to live and live in peace. Director Jones, shall become the new leader of DARPA and the robotic engineering scientists will be on board giving one of their own an appropriate amount of time to heal. Whit and Shu shall find the other special ones that posses similar gifts to form a new DARPA with their help. Transportation will be provided by the military wherever they need to go including different parts of the world. The dates are set for these conferences to begin where different countries will be attending in the discussions. A full list of important subjects will be reviewed including how the human race and the creatures of Earth can live together without causing extinction to many species. Another important subject is how to minimize further deterioration of our planet.

CHAPTER 7

A worldwide memorial needs to take place televising the victims in many regions to serve as a reminder of humanity's mistakes. A memorial plague shall bear the heroes names that stopped further darkness from taking over our world. The locations, dates, times, are set for the international conferences to begin, the locations are as follows, in a unknown location in the great state of Texas the first conference takes place, the second, somewhere in the desert in Nevada. As previously mentioned a worldwide memorial has been televising in many regions on oversized screens called Jumbotron. Exactly, one week later the memorial service has begun and everyone was in attendance Director Jones, Whit, Shu, Marcus, Julie, their twin daughters, three of the robotic engineering scientists only, Jon Tan Lan, Sam Andre Dame, Tim Von Gleason. The scientist that wasn't in attendance is Ron Ben Ruckman, everybody there knows how much pain he is in losing his pregnant wife in the blast. Many other military personnel are also in attendance, a full military service salute is part of the memorial service ceremony. This memorial service ceremony location is Indianapolis, Indiana, perfect location because it already has two military bases and it's 559.1 miles away from Virginia. A memorial plague is covered and soon it will be removed for many to visit the site, on the plague it bears the names of the heroes that gave their lives to stop a greater darkness from continuing throughout our world. When the cover is removed the writing on it says the following, (These special individual's began in darkness, but afterwards gave the ultimate sacrifice to save our world from complete darkness to light becoming heroes in the process and acts of bravery), may their names be known (Terrence Johnson, Soldaat) supreme leader. (Allic, Tijo, Imon, Tiro, Ison, Fuge), known as the six points of order, the six regional leaders. Director Jones speaks, today heavy tears are shed and great souls will be missed, may God lead DARPA to a brighter future bringing visions and salvation to our deteriorating world. Let us be guided by humbleness and join together as one for the entire human race and the creatures of our precious Earth. After the memorial service ceremony many from the group try contacting their colleague scientist Ron Ben Ruckman, but it's like he disappeared.

Chapter 8

The actual events of his disappearance will be revealed soon, in the meantime, the important DARPA conferences are scheduled in a couple of days in a unknown location in the great state of Texas. Before the DARPA conferences begin which are a series of conferences in different locations worldwide, and the sole purpose of these conferences is to implement immediate solutions to salvage our world from extinction. Events that took place with scientist Ron Ben Ruckman, upon being informed that his pregnant wife is among the victims that were killed in the blast. As shown, he was escorted by the military psychologists and healthcare personnel to the lobby where it has comfortable seating and the staff tried their best to comfort him. The scientist wouldn't stop crying and was extremely hurt inside, he didn't show any sign of aggression or hatred. The scientist colleagues were still in a important meeting with military personnel being briefed of current events and how to proceed forward with the upcoming DARPA conferences. Afterwards, the scientist Ron Ben Ruckman told the military psychologist and healthcare personnel he needed to get some fresh air and walk around to clear his mind. At this point, there was no reason to hold him or detain him, the scientist actually called a taxi and just took off to a nearby bar. Somehow, he had money with him it is not sure how maybe he secretly kept money in case of an emergency. When the taxi dropped him off he started getting hammered drinking alcohol his eyes were red from crying so much and deep inside he was hurting really bad. While he was drinking a man approached him and started drinking with him, little did he know that individual was radicalized extremists far beyond the origins of Islam, the hatred towards modern technologies and advancements changing mankind's ancestry. It didn't take long for their opinions to match, for starters the scientist blames DARPA with all it's advanced technologies directly for what happened to his pregnant wife that broke him inside. The mysterious man was part of something much greater, he was part of an Islamic group that were getting ready to leave on a freighter cargo ship docked off the coast of Texas and was getting ready to travel somewhere in the Middle East. The mysterious man told the scientist that he can be part of something much greater then the modern world, a true leader of what our world should be written in scriptures throughout history. At this time, they both took off in a vehicle that was later found in flames, and even the small boat that headed out towards the freighter cargo ship called (TRITTON). The small boat a small explosive device detonated sinking it to the bottom after both men boarded the freighter cargo ship. As you can imagine, after the scientist didn't return after many hours, a full investigation from the military was under effect.

CHAPTER 9

Investigators, followed every single track of the scientist, they found the taxi driver and interrogated him, they went to the bar and interrogated the bartender. They found the car in flames, later on they even found the small boat at the bottom of the ocean, but it was already to late the freighter cargo ship (TRITTON), had left towards the Middle East in a very dangerous part of the world. During their voyage the mysterious man revealed himself his name is Issac, he called the scientist Ben which was his first name. Issac told Ben that he is destined to be a great leader, and introduces him to his fellow comrades, everyone there knew the Ben the scientist has great knowledge and wisdom of the modern world. They all gather together reading scriptures and teaching Ben how their ancestors had great visions for our world. Little by little Ben the scientist is becoming a radicalized extremists with a mind that can truly cause major damage. Conspiracy theories among the military investigators are possible scenarios, first, the scientist was targeted by a radicalized extremists group. Second, the mysterious man somehow drugged the scientist that impaired his thinking process actually enhancing his inner emotions, turning them into hatred and hopelessness. Further investigation, revealed that the tracking device the scientist had inside his body was removed and disposed of, the only conclusion is that it was removed surgically.

CHAPTER 10

Further investigation, also revealed that no fingerprints of any kind were identified anywhere this only means one thing that they are dealing with a very professional group. While, all these developments were taking place, the extremely important DARPA conferences begin. The DARPA conference brings environmentalists, conservationists, urban farmers, architects, agronomists, public health experts, among other specialists all over the world. The future of DARPA and the world as we know it will be formed in these discussions, so many countries from all over the world are here with representatives. The discussions begin, first, on the agenda is transforming are world with hydroponics-mineral nutrition solutions in a water solvent. Second, aquaponics-aquatic creatures, fish and sails to cultivate plants in water. Third, aeroponics-grows plants in the air, these advanced methods of farming must be implemented at a worldwide level especially in areas most needed. Next, on the agenda is the reduction of meats, poultry, and all types of seafood, worldwide. Let us breakdown solutions, first, is to eliminate commercialization of these animals and sea creatures, instead, everyone on Earth should reduce this demand and supplement it with grains, beans, vegetables, fruits, and other alternatives worldwide. Second, eliminate hunting any type of land species on Earth, eliminate recreational and commercial fishing. Third, our oceans will have protection zones and international waters will be ratified to protect sea creatures from becoming extinct. Forth, all hotels with an abundance of land, farms with many acres not in production, agriculture and ranches with tons of acres not in production should all share with Earth's land species, having appropriate barriers for safety. These measures must be implemented worldwide to salvage our Earth creatures from becoming extinct, DARPA and other personal shall assist in this future goal. Furthermore, the robotic engineering scientists team shall join other experts worldwide to create this goal. We are also assigning Whit and Shu to recruit other special ones around the world to take charge of this goal, the cadets will be assisting them also.

CHAPTER 11

We now bring how to supplement the food sources in a realistic dialogue, we begin with the land animals. Since, the demand of meats, and poultry, will be much less we will transform many plants into other sources of food. We will do the same thing with all types of seafood, the demand itself will be much less and many businesses will sell other sources of food that grow from the ground. Our entire mentality throughout our world must focus more on our survival and halting the extinction of ourselves and Earth's creatures. Throughout our schools and in every region everyone we be taught how important this is and receive assistance to make this goal possible. Severe penalties will be in place for the trafficking of any exotic or wild creatures both land and sea whether it's sell, consumption, pets, especially in black underground markets. The sacrifices and hardships we face in our world now will be how our future will be determined. Now, we carefully move to halt further deterioration of our world, we will breakdown solutions also. First, make a worldwide transition to eliminate all gas and diesel powered vehicles to electrical or hydrogen powered, trade in equal to clean up the population. Second, eliminate so many cars worldwide and supplement an advance transit autonomous train system, autonomous bus transport, and all other transport systems, reducing populations significantly. Third, these transport systems can be adopted to existing highways and roads with minimum construction, security in terminals and on every transport systems. Fourth, introduction of other advance technologies for transport such as, trains, buses, commercial planes, private planes, adaptations can also be done for cargo ships, recreational boats, tractor trailers, commercial trucks. Fifth, starting immediately, all commercial and private properties apply solar powered systems to assist the current power grid worldwide. Sixth, many companies and governments can achieve this goal assorting out all challenges ahead, this move will significantly reduce pollution. Seventh, supplement coal, and other harmful energy sources with alternative energies, transitioning the industry with alternative energies. In many cases sending experts to make this transition possible, companies learning how alternative energies work with assistance to make change the industry and provide employment in their communities. Finally, implement worldwide coordination with many governments by bringing solutions mapping out charts and calculations how much of an emergency this is, many countries have experienced severe changes to our world already and we as a planet must take action immediately to prevent further deterioration.

Chapter 12

These DARPA conferences continued after this conference the next one was scheduled the same week in a unknown location in the desert of Nevada. Then the DARPA conferences moves to different locations in Asia, and Europe, both in unknown locations, the security apparatus in these DARPA conferences are at the highest levels. While, these DARPA conferences are presently taking place, another event is happening in the most religious sites on Earth. What started as a small gathering grew into massive numbers of protests around the globe. Let's review carefully exactly what is happening, what locations, for what purpose, and if there is any answers to what religious groups are saying holding up signs everywhere. Ever since, the massive explosion that took so many lives and at the time Earth's energy grid was completely paralyzed when the Massive Space Energy Sphere left our atmosphere, continuing beyond our galaxy to the farthest regions in space. At first, small groups of religious groups were holding signs everywhere in every part of our world, challenging the origins of the Massive Space Energy Sphere. Let's breakdown these sites carefully, in Israel, in the city of Jerusalem, the old city of Jerusalem christian quarter. Christianity and Judaism in the thousands and everyday more are gathering, all of them are holding signs saying (it's Jesus as the Son of God), (the return of Jesus Christ), (it's the one transcendent God). In Italy, Vatican City, a city-state surrounded by Rome, headquarters of the Roman Catholic church. Catholics in the the thousands more are gathering everyday, many are holding signs saying (The Holy Bible is being revealed), (the return of Christ). In France, Lourdes, thousands of Catholics are holding similar signs and more are gathering everyday. In the United Kingdom, in Stonehenge, thousands are gathered holding different similar signs, all challenging the origins of the Massive Space Energy Sphere.

Chapter 13

In Czech Republic, Spanish Synagogue, Jewish people are in the thousands more and more are gathering everyday. All of them are holding signs saying (believe in Torah), (the whole of laws given to Israelites), (In India, Kashi Vishwanath Temple, many thousands of Hindu people are gathered more are gathering everyday. All of them are holding signs saying (Brahman universal soul of God), (Atman is part of Brahman in everyone), (Brahman takes many forms). In India, Mahabodhi Temple Buddhists pilgrimage, many thousands of Buddhists are gathered holding signs saying (the path to enlightenment is here), (practice, development of morality, meditation, and wisdom). In India, Ghats Of Varanasi, many thousands are gathered holding similar signs challenging the origins of the Massive Space Energy Sphere. In India, Boudhanath, Nepal, Buddhists in the thousands are gathered with more approaching many holding similar signs challenging the origins of the Massive Space Energy Sphere. In Bhutan, Taktsang, South Asia, Buddhist monastery many thousands of Buddhists are gathered with more joining everyday holding similar signs challenging the origins of the Massive Space Energy Sphere. In Indonesia, Borobudur, Buddhist Temple, many gather in the thousands more and more are joining everyday holding similar signs challenging the origins of the Massive Space Energy Sphere. In Thailand, Wat Rong Khun, Buddha's purity, thousands are gathered everywhere more everyday many holding similar signs challenging the origins of the Massive Space Energy Sphere. In Cambodia, Angkor Wat, Hinduism and Buddhism, in the thousands gathered with more approaching everyday all holding different types of similar signs challenging the origins of the Massive Space Energy Sphere.

CHAPTER 14

In Australia, Uluru, the Aboriginal Pitjantjatjara people in the thousands gather holding signs saying (our ancestors have returned), (the dreamtime has returned). In Australia, Uluru-Kata Tjuta national park, the Yankunytjatjara and Pitjantjatjara people in the thousands are gathered everywhere holding similar signs challenging the origins of the Massive Space Energy Sphere. In Africa, Victoria Falls, Zambia and Zimbabwe, a vast majority of Christianity, Roman Catholic, Anglican, Apostolic, Methodist, Baptist, Seventh Day Adventist, Presbyterian, Salvation Army Devotees, gather in overwhelming numbers in the thousands all holding different types of signs all challenging the origins of the Massive Space Energy Sphere. In Africa, Ethiopia, Rock-Hewn Churches Of Lalibela, Ethiopian Christianity believers are gathered in unprecedented numbers in the thousands holding many signs saying (Son of God has returned), (king of Kings Jesus Christ). In Iran, Nasir Al-Mulk Mosque, Iranian Muslims gather everywhere thousands of thousands with more arriving everyday many are holding signs saying (the Quran in Arabic is the final unaltered revelation of God), (the prophets Adam, Abraham, Moses, and Jesus, have revealed themselves). In Saudi Arabia, Mecca, mostly Sunni Muslims with Shia and other foreigners, in the thousands of thousands with more arriving everyday many are holding signs saying (one God Mohammed as his prophet), (the Hajj prophet Ibrahim), (Kaaba dedicated to the one God). In Egypt, Mount Sinai, Jewish, Christian, and Islamic faiths, in the thousands of thousands gather everywhere many holding different types of signs challenging the Massive Space Energy Sphere. In Egypt, Abu Simbel Temples, Egyptians Muslims, In the thousands of thousands a mixture of ancient pagan beliefs, monotheistic religions, and a small minority of Jews, and Christians, are gathered many are holding different types of signs challenging the origins of the Massive Space Energy Sphere. In Wyoming, Devils Tower, known as Lakota Sioux as Mató Tipila "Bears' Lodge", in the thousands of thousands, Protestant, Christian, Catholic, Mormon, Jewish, Eastern religion, Atheist, Agnostic, Scientology, New Age, Taoism, Theology, ZEN, LDS, are holding many different types of signs challenging the origins of the Massive Space Energy Sphere. Many American Indian tribes are also holding signs saying (that's God's altar), (Denali, "The High One"), displaying traditional sun-dance rituals. In Mexico, Cenote Sagrado, portals with the Gods, (Well Of Sacrifice), Pre-Columbian Maya Archaeological site. maya rain god Chaac, Maya civilization child sacrifice was practised as a means of petitioning the rain god Chaac for continuity of supply to ensure their crops would thrive. Today, the Yucatan península is largely Christian they have adopted Catholic icons to represent the holiness these sites had in pre-hispanic times. Thousands upon thousands of Christians and modern day Maya, are gathered everywhere many holding signs challenging the origins of the Massive Space Energy Sphere. Modern day Maya still live of their old empire in Central America, Belize, Honduras, El Salvador, Guatemala, and five states in Mexico.

CHAPTER 15

While all these religious protesting chaos is happening across the world it brings up yet another type of conference. Astronomers, Physicists, Astrophysicists, from different countries, even high ranking military officials from DARPA Space Force. In Canada, at the university of Toronto, the discussions will include recent data collection, developments in space, life form theories, and answers all possibilities. The conferences will take place in Canada because of ocean sea level rise in many coastal areas and some lost of livable habitants in other land región areas. Everything has been arranged the first conference will take place in a few days, preparations are made for the conference and security is at a elevated level. Everyone is arriving and they are all very much aware of the religious protests that are taking place worldwide in many religious sites. The emergency conference begins, in the height of all the religious protests some DARPA Space Force officials are present, despite the DARPA conferences which are undergoing the future of our world. DARPA Space Force reveals that their satellite attempted a sample of the invisible microscopic cerebrum molecules, which nothing is known so far. The findings were completely inconclusive meaning somehow the unknown origins retracted back into the quarter sphere. Not leaving any traces of anything suggests that we are dealing with invisible living microscopic cerebrum molecules. DARPA Space Force is extremely secretive but sharing classified information with other nations brings different point of views and solutions. Now, the Astronomers, Physicists, Astrophysicists, take over in these important conversations. Let's bring all points of views, let's begin with what we know so far about our universe. Roughly 68% of the universe is Dark Energy, Dark Matter makes up about 27%, the rest everything on Earth. Everything ever observed with all of our instruments all normal matter adds up to less than 5% of the universe. Different theories, cosmological constant, Quantum theory new kind of dynamical energy, fluid or field named (Quintessence). First, it is dark, meaning it's not in forms of stars and planets, second, it's not form of dark clouds of normal matter, matter made up of particles called Baryons. Third, dark matter is not antimatter, because we do not see the unique gamma rays that are produced when antimatter annihilates with matter. Finally, baryonic matter could still make up the dark matter if it were all tied up in brown dwarfs or in small, dense chunks of heavy elements. These possibilities are known as massive compact halo objects, or (MACHOs). The most common view is that dark matter is not baryonic at all, it is made up of other more exotic particles like axions or wimps (weakly interacting massive particles).

CHAPTER 16

Now, we move forward with what is the most powerful thing in the universe, gamma-ray burst (GRBs), and Fermi Paradox. Astronomers all agree the most powerful thing in our universe are called gamma ray bursts (GRBs). This occurs when stars 150 times the size of our sun explode, producing the brightest light sources in the universe. Releasing so much energy in a few seconds equal to our sun can produce over a lifetime of 10 billion years. The same amount of energy in 10 trillion billion megaton bombs, scientists conclude, GRBs could be killing our changes of ever discovering life on other planets. Further study show GRBs are sterilizing the cosmos, GRBs are stunning burst of radiation consisting of beams of gamma radiation lasting seconds to a few minutes but some last a few hours. Hypernovae are a more spectacular version of the better-known supernova, a massive explosion of light and energy that occurs when a high-mass star implodes. When this occurs, the explosion launches massive amounts of harmful gamma radiation into space at very high speeds. GRBs occur every 100,000 to one million years in a single galaxy, the Milky Way galaxy has never experienced a GRB. The most likely candidate for a GRB in our galaxy is about 7,500 light years away, a safe distance from Earth but close enough to be bright enough that night will seem like day. After carefully reviewing our universe now we enter (Kardashev Scale), and theories of possibilities of civilizations throughout the universe. Let's begin, the human race isn't even on this scale yet, since we still sustain our energy needs from dead planets and animals, here on Earth, we are a lowly type 0 civilization. The human race has a long way to go before being promoted to a type 1 civilization, all things considered, we will reach type 1 in 100-200 years time. A type 1 designation is a given to species who have been able to harness all the energy that is available from a neighboring star. Gathering and storing it to meet the energy demands of a growing population, the human race would need to boost our current energy production over 100,000 times to reach this status. To harness all Earth's energy means control over all natural forces, such as, volcanoes, the weather, and even earthquakes! (in theory). It's hard to believe, but compared to advances not developed, these are basic and primitive levels of control (please note, this is nothing compared to the capabilities of societies with higher rankings). Type 2 civilization-harness the power of an entire star (not transforming starlight into energy, but controlling the star). Most popular is the (hypothetical, Dyson Sphere), this device, would encompass every single inch of the star. Gathering most or all of its energy output and transferring it to a planet for later use.

Chapter 17

If fusion power (the mechanism that powers stars) is mastered by the race, a reactor on a immense scale could be used to satisfy their needs. Nearby gas giants can be utilized for their hydrogen, slowly drained of life by an orbiting reactor. Scenario factors-what would so much energy mean for any species, well, nothing known to science could wipe out a type 2 civilization. If the human race survives long enough to reach this status, if a moon sized object entered our solar system on a collision course with Earth we'd have the ability to vaporize it out of existence. On the other hand, we could move Earth out of the way, completely dodging it, how about we didn't want to move Earth, are there any other options. How about having the capability of moving Jupiter, or any other planet into the way to counter the force of impact. Now, the human race has gone from having control over a planet, to a star, this has resulted in us harboring enough (disposable energy) to essentially make our civilization immune to extinction. Type 3 civilization-a species becomes galactic traversers with knowledge of everything having to do with energy. Becoming a master race, human terminalogy, through hundreds of thousands of years of evolution both biological and mechanical. Results, in the inhabitants of this type 3 civilization, being incredibly different from the human race as we know it. Cyborgs (or cybernetic organism, beings both biological and robotic). Descendants of regular human beings a sub-species among the now-highly advanced society. Biological humans would be seen as being disabled, inferior, or unevolved by their cybernetic counterparts. At this stage, humans would have developed colonies of robots that are capable of (self replication) their population may increase into the millions spreading throughout the galaxy. Colonizing star after star, with intelligence to build Dyson Spheres to encapsulate each one. Creating a huge network with capabilities to carry energy back to the home planet. Expanding over the galaxy in this manner, brings other challenges, mostly, the species would be constrained by the laws of physics. First, is light-speed travel, unless they develop a working warp drive. Second, use that immaculate energy cache to master wormhole teleportation. Both remain theoretical but developments are being made. Type 4 civilization-astronomers, physicists and astrophysicist debate over if type 4 civilization is even possible. Some believe beyond type 3 is to advanced, others believe that a further level can be achieved. Type 4 civilizations would be able to harness the energy content of the entire universe. They could traverse the accelerating expansion of space, advance races of these species may live inside supermassive black holes. By passing previous methods of generating energy, these intellectual feats are considered impossible. A type 4 civilization needs to tap into energy sources unknown to humans using strange, or currently unknown, laws of physics. Type 5 civilization might be the next advancement to such a civilization. Here beings would be like gods, having intelligence to manipulate the universe at will. Human knowledge is far from reaching this status, debates have been made whether it's possible and the answers are to preserve planet Earth. Extinguish wars, continue to support scientific advances and discoveries.

CHAPTER 18

After all the discussions are made, analysts are presented, theories are made, even developments from every point of view, the conclusion is as follows. DARPA Space Force, NASA, will join many other countries in further study of space exploration in search of unknown origins and life form possibilities. We shall make announcements worldwide on our partnerships and will continue to find answers to the unknown, giving our world hope to very difficult questions. We will try our best to calm the worldwide religious protesters and give them reports of any findings in the near future. Everyone knows that the answers are extremely difficult but our joint efforts in space exploration should bring very much needed answers to calm down our civilizations on Earth. As the emergency conference comes to a conclusion, the DARPA conferences are making a lot of progress. We will now carefully breakdown each worldwide agreements and progress by pinpointing global concerns with innovative methods by using all future developments and technologies to salvage our planet Earth. Each global problem is extremely difficult and the decision making can be harsh but the ultimate goal is to stop the further deterioration of our planet Earth. Let's begin with (human growth populations) estimated human growth presently 7.775 billion. In 2040 and 2050 estimated to be between 8 to 10.5 billion, in 2050 and on estimated to be 9.8 billion, and finally in 2100 estimated to be 11.2 billion human beings on Earth. The world's governments have all agreed that this problem is not sustainable and have broken down four phase levels to counteract this global problem. Phase one-male contraception pills, educating girls, removing barriers to contraception, challenging assumptions about family size and contraception, alleviating poverty, exercise the choice, having a smaller family, women's rights, myth busting. Phase two-delayed marriages, medical facilities, legislative actions, providing incentives, spread awareness, women empowerment, eradicate poverty, education, easy and cheap availability of contraceptives, development. Phase three-war, contraception, abstinence, abortion, pornography, sterilization, one-child and two-child policies, family planning, migration from rural areas to urban areas, emigration. Phase four critical-the legalization of abortion, financial incentives for countries to increase their abortion, sterilization and contraception-use rates, indoctrination of children, mandatory population control and coercion of other forms, such as withdrawing disaster and food aid unless an LDC implements population control programs. Effective immediately, these four phases will be activated throughout our world in efforts to slowdown the human growth rates agreed upon all developed nations and mandated to all other countries.

CHAPTER 19

Next on the agenda is (food supply for future generations), DARPA has teamed up with many scientists, biologists, and other experts worldwide to solve this massive problem. The latest innovations are at the frontier of solving this problem, let's begin, creating autonomous robot farming, presenting precious dirt, giving waste a second chance, slowing the aging process, making smarter choices, improve honeybee health, how farming in forests could sustain the planet, why food's plastic problem is bigger than we realize, solution-non-biodegradable plastic, how farming can help to heal nature. How to fix our broken food system, solutions-wild chick pea plants, "bee vectoring", drones, education. Alternative crops-such as Kedondong, seawater to grow food-in the desert, the wild seeds that could save civilization. Putting phosphorus back into the soil in Africa, compost can restore the soil structure by adding organic matter. Compost comes from organic waste, it's not only valuable, but accessible. Cattle and other livestock release anthropogenic greenhouse gas emissions, solutions-altering the diet eaten could reduce methane, putting additives into animal feed, vaccination. Using seawater and solar power for agriculture, solutions-triple axle-food production, water scarcity, and renewable energy, hothouse, pipe dream, siphon water from the Red Sea to the Dead Sea. Honeybees could help protect wildlife, grow food and make money. Solutions-80% of elephants that approached the trail farms were kept out, if beekeeping can protect honeybee populations. Provide critical pollination services, help with wildlife restoration and protection and be sustainable. A wave of new technology could help the industry overcome it's challenges, (HUCHIHIVE) to start collating information and provide a tech-based approach to improve beekeeping. The bold, tech-fueled plan to save Africa's big beasts. Solutions-putting a GPS-enabled collars, tourist drives economy and jobs, brings government support. The Domain Awareness System (DAS) software solution, the map compiles data like wildlife locations, rangers and vehicles, sites of past poaching incursions, weather and more, tracking software.

CHAPTER 20

How to sustainably feed 10 billion people by 2050, one-reduce food loss and waste, two-shift to healthier, more sustainable diets. Three-avoid competition from bio energy for food crops and land, four-achieve replacement-level fertility rates. Five-increase livestock and pasture productivity, six-improve crop breeding, seven-improve soil and water management. eight-plant existing cropland more frequently, nine-adapt to climate change, ten-link productivity gains with protection of natural ecosystems. Eleven-limit inevitable cropland expansion to lands with low environmental opportunity costs. Twelve-reforest agriculture lands with little intensification potential, thirteen-conserve and restore peatlands. Fourteen-improve wild fisheries management, fifteen-improve productivity and environmental performance of aquaculture. Sixteen-reduce enteric fermentation through new technologies, seventeen-reduce emissions through improved manure management. Eighteen-reduce emissions from manure left on pasture, nineteen-reduce emissions from fertilizers by increasing nitrogen use efficiency. Twenty-adopt emissions-reducing rice management and varieties, twenty one-increase agricultural energy efficiency and shift to non-fossil energy sources. Twenty two-implement realistic options to sequester carbon in soils. Next, on the agenda is how to deal with the world's rubbish, which has become a giant problem. In 2010 3.5 million tonnes of rubbish per day, by 2100 that amount will triple, recycling 43% plastic waste ends up in landfills, 20 million tonnes fill our oceans. Solutions-converting rubbish into pavement for public roads, trash is burnt and converted to electricity, pulverize e-waste into microscopic nano particles, garage clinical insurance-recyclable bits in exchange for money toward healthcare. Next, is possibly the greatest challenge of all energy for future generations.

CHAPTER 21

To tackle this overwhelming problem DARPA will coordinate with other countries to come up with the greatest innovations of future technologies similar to what was achieved in the (ISS) International Space Station, where great contributions came from many countries on Earth. Many more countries will join these efforts to resolve these challenges and salvage our planet from further deterioration. Solar power stations in space could supply the world with limitless energy, many scientists maintain that giant, space-based solar farms could provide an environmentally-friendly answer to the world's energy crisis. The sun always shines in space, an orbital solar power station is seen as an inexhaustible source of clean energy. Photovoltaic array is composed of a lightweight, deployable structure made of many smaller "solar satellites" that could easily connect together in space to form much larger array and "harvest sunlight". This approach also makes assembly, maintenance and repair considerably easier. This completed array would orbit about 22,000 miles above the Earth and "beam" the energy back down to the surface. The photovoltaic array converts the sunlight into electricity, which in turn is converted into RF electrical power (microwaves) that are beamed wirelessly to ground-based receivers. This would take the form of giant wire nets measuring up to four miles across that could be installed across deserts or farmlands or even over lakes. A solar facility like this could generate a constant flow of 2,000 gigawatts of power. The microwaves that transmit the energy to the surface would be at the so-called non-ionizing radiation frequency. Electromagnetic radiation can pass through the Earth's atmosphere, including clouds and weather, without interruption, without interference. Harvesting renewable energy from the sun and outer space at the same time.

CHAPTER 22

Present future energy scenarios-by 2040 projections of the primary global energy consumption by fuel. Coal consumption would increase or remain flat under half of the scenarios described here. Natural gas consumption will grow under every scenario, while liquids consumption will grow in all but two scenarios. The share of nuclear power is highest under ambitious climate scenarios. Renewable energy, led by wind and solar power, grow rapidly, though they primarily add to, rather than displace. Fossil fuels unless more ambitious climate policies are put into place. Emissions concerns, economic growth, demand, and trade, will mean difficult policy choices for national governments and energy majors. These decisions will come to define the globe's future energy landscape. The alternative energy sources of the future-space-based solar, human power, tidal power, hydrogen power, magma power, nuclear waste, embeddable solar power, algae power, flying wind power, fusion power. The future of energy that could help save our planet-the limitations of green energy, fusion power, sewage as power, sunshine-powered water purifier, desolenator power, eco-homes, people power, energy from exercise, energy floors, charge your phone with your clothes, solar-powered clothing. Great success has been achieved at the DARPA conferences, addressing the most important issues of our time which will directly improve our planet from further deterioration. With agreements among the nations of our world the following achievements will become a reality effective immediately.

CHAPTER 23

First, eliminating gas and diesel powered vehicles, second, eliminate so many cars, introduce advance transit autonomous trains and bus transport. Third, adopted to existing highways and roads, fourth, introduce advance technologies to trains, buses, commercial planes, private planes, cargo ships, recreational boats, tractor trailers, commercial trucks, fifth, solar powered systems (eco-friendly) to all commercial and private properties. (UNI-WORLD) will undergo a total transformation in different regions of our world. Once built only for Earth's creatures that are on the brink of extinction, now, (UNI-WORLD) shall be shared with humans, beautiful eco-luxurious hotels will be built on many sites. The goal is for humans and Earth's creatures to interact in peaceful environments. Of course, safe barriers will be put in place to protect the guest, the hyper-loop eco-train system will still be the main source of traveling throughout (UNI-WORLD) with the exception of other regions. Zon's memorial plaque will be placed at all entrances of (UNI-WORLD) to honor his dreams and visions. Both Whit and Shu in coordination with DARPA, using a passenger plane to travel to different regions around the world to find the other special ones. They also posses special telepathic abilities to communicate with Earth's creatures. With the leaderships of Whit and Shu, these groups of special ones will work closely with the cadets in different (UNI-WORLD) locations. Humans around the world can interact with Earth's creatures learning and experiencing how vital of a role they play in our ecosystems and our very existence.

CHAPTER 24

With plenty of lands and oceans hopefully, humans and Earth's creatures can learn to coexist for many futures to come without fear of extinction. Domesticated animals will remain the same and wild creatures some require barriers from entering human environments. Nations worldwide have also agreed on strict penalties for violators which can include fines, imprisonment depending on how severe the violations are. The main goal is education and rehabilitation to the majority, better understanding brings better awareness. While all these conferences and religious protest were taking place in a series of events in different parts of the world and at different times, something else was also taking place in a unknown location that has a more sinister outcome. The rise of ancient prophecy something far from anything known to mankind, something that will change our world forever, something that nightmares are multiplied many times over. One of the greatest scientific minds of our generation is being groomed into a direct descendent to God. Radicalized by extremists beyond our modern world concepts, to understand how did we get to this point I will carefully breakdown everything that led to this nightmare. Let's begin, going back to the cargo ship (TRITTON), where scientist Ron Ben Ruckman has joined an extremely dangerous radicalized extremist group where Issac and his fellow comrades are teaching Ben the scientist ancient scriptures. Ron Ben Ruckman families bloodline is Muslim and he has devoted his entire life to modern science. When he heard that his pregnant wife (Eva) was killed by the most horrific incident on American soil it took his soul.

Chapter 25

Now, little by little his mental transformation begins, afterwards it will be revealed exactly where they are headed and what is the greater purpose. First, let's start what his mind has previously known so far then begin the mental transformation from the ancient scriptures. Before the transformation-terminology-science is defined as the pursuit of knowledge and understanding of the natural and social world following systematic methodology based on empiricism. Experimentation and methodological naturalism, organized body of knowledge human beings have gained by research. Scientific investigation needs to adhere scientific method, a process evaluating empirical knowledge that explains observable events without recourse to supernatural notions. The transformation-from the ancient doctrines hours and hours turned into days after days, this continued into weeks after weeks, then months have passed. The mental transformation of a modern scientist slowly turned into the mind of a great messiah (a direct descendant to God). Islam has it's own world view system including beliefs about "ultimate reality, epistemology, ontology, ethics, and purpose. Islam, nature is not seen as something separate but as an integral part of a holistic outlook on God. (And follow not that of which you have not the (certain) knowledge of …1736). (Say: bring your proof if you are truthful 2:111), both in matters of theological belief and in natural science.

CHAPTER 26

Traditional ulema efforts to formulate systematic explanation of natural phenomenon with "natural laws". Such laws were blasphemous because they limit "God's freedom to act" a principle enshired in aya 14:4: God sendeth whom he will astray, and guideth whom he will,"which (they believed) applied to all of creation not just humanity. The Quran abounds with "scientific facts" among these miracles are "everything, from relativity, quantum mechanics, Big Bang theory, black holes and pulsars, genetics, embryology, modern geology, thermodynamics, even the laser and hydrogen fuel cells. Modern science as corrupt foreign thought, it's incompatible with Islamic teachings, the only remedy is strict Islamic teachings. Real enlightenment the complete adoption of modern science, the only remedy the mastery of modern science and the replacement of the religious worldview by scientific worldview. They praised the attempts of western scientists for the discovery of the secrets of nature. They warned against various empiricist and materialistic interpretations of scientific findings. Scientific knowledge can reveal certain aspects of the physical world, but it should not be identified with the alpha and omega of knowledge. Rather, it has to be integrated into a metaphysical framework-consistent with the Muslim worldview-in which higher levels of knowledge are recognized and the role of science in bringing us closer to God is fulfilled.

CHAPTER 27

Meanwhile, somewhere in the former Soviet Union Uzbeks, Chataev, and other Russian-speaking terrorist are well organized and planning a much sinister global vision. The post-Soviet world can travel easier with Syrian or Yemeni passports, bringing the greater vision with them. Militants in Syria, are winning over many Rohingya with their vision of global struggle for Islam. Religious Muslims in Kazakhstan, Tajikistan, and Uzbekistan, in untold numbers are attractive targets for radicals for new recruits. Several popular Sheikhs Saudi cleric Abdulaziz al-Tarefe, now have significant Russian-Arabic-language followings on social media. Providing passports to radicals from Caucasus, Russian Kavkaz, mountain system and region lying between the Black Sea (west) and the Caspian Sea (east) occupied by Russia, Georgia, Azerbaijan and Armenia. With ideologies that it is much easier to allow would-be jihadis leave the country than dealing with this overwhelming threat at home. Future predictions have terrorist attacks more likely coming from the East than the Middle East. Nevertheless, this overwhelming vision has grown to unprecedented levels joining many regions and now prophecy is about to be fulfilled. The cause is embedded in all their souls, no one on Earth really knows the nightmare that is about to unfold. After months pass, the mind of one of the greatest scientific minds has completely been transformed into ancient prophecy. I want to make it abundantly clear, that even though the ancient doctrines hates modern technologies. The weaponry they possess is state of the art sophisticated anti-missile system including aircraft, drones, whatever is necessary. They have acquired these weapons in the underground market using untold amounts of money. They know that modern nations won't hesitate to destroy their global vision especially DARPA.

CHAPTER 28

It is believed that former DARPA scientist Ron Ben Ruckman was targeted by radical extremists. Taking advantage of his vulnerability state of mind from grieving the lost of his beloved pregnant wife (Eva), the gender of the baby was not known because they wanted everything to be a surprise. Be warned, the following events will reshape our world as we know it, even though the efforts by DARPA and the world nations are to be recognized. It is believed that the freighter cargo ship (TRITTON) took voyage somewhere in the Islamic world, where prophecy has delivered their beloved Messiah a direct descendant of God, has been fulfilled. DARPA has satellites throughout space, and those satellites picked up a transmission in Russian-Arabic-language, that nightmares are made of. This transmission received the highest levels and was translated in several languages which called an emergency meeting at DARPA. The following takes place at DARPA's conference room, with Director Jones, military personnel, team of robotic engineering scientists, and other experts. Keep in mind, Whit and Shu are busy coordinating with the other special ones and cadets the reopening of (UNI-WORLD) in different regions around the world. The following transmission was received by DARPA's satellites and other nation satellites, the exact pinpoint of location is inconclusive due to many factors. One factor, can be electronic warfare (EW) jammers, other state of the art devices can also be used. Despite, these factors the DARPA satellites pick up the transmission. Inside the conference room at DARPA, let's begin with the transmission translated in english. I stand here today, not as a human and a robotic engineer scientist called Ron Ben Ruckman. I stand here today, as the great ancient visionary from old scriptures. I stand here today, to embrace the ancient teachings and recreate the world we should be living. I stand here today, a sworn enemy of the modern world with all it's advancements and technologies. I stand here today, as a direct descendant of our Creator. I stand here today, as your supreme leader to fulfill ancient prophecy. I stand here today, with the spirit of the Creator and my beloved children. I stand here today, for this day to be written and remembered in history.

Chapter 29

After listening to a very powerful speech everyone in the conference room at DARPA (which the new headquarters is located in a unknown location in Texas) they all looked at each other saying what has just happened. Director Jones, briefs the rest of the team and tells them that was our fellow scientist Ron Ben Ruckman which is now the enemy of our world. Maybe, one day we can get to him and try to save his life if not we need to prepare with the rest of our nations on very sophisticated attacks that will come from the mind of a great scientific mind. Director Jones, continues saying we will coordinate with other nations to put in place emergency measures to protect us from these attacks. Almost everyone in the team is in complete shock and can't believe the realization of their fellow scientist and friend. Military doctors and psychologist are here to help us cope with these unfortunate events to help us move forward with all the advancements we have achieved at the DARPA conferences.

Chapter 30

Conclusion-it took almost the extinction of many of Earth's creatures and the lost of habitable lands. Due to the deterioration of our tiny planet called Earth, for nations to reach one conclusion to join forces to stop whatever the human race was currently doing. In order, to put in place laws and practices to salvage what is left. Now, our world faces another real threat that is beginning to grow the (NEW ORDER).